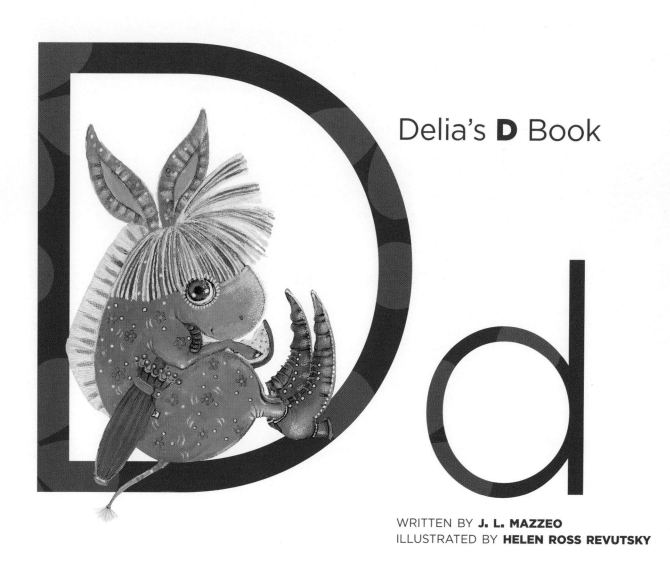

Delia's **D** Book

WRITTEN BY **J. L. MAZZEO**
ILLUSTRATED BY **HELEN ROSS REVUTSKY**

dingles&company New Jersey

First Printing

Published By dingles&company
P.O. Box 508
Sea Girt, New Jersey 08750

LIBRARY OF CONGRESS CATALOG CARD NUMBER
2005928855
ISBN
1-59646-434-8

Printed in the United States of America

My Letter Library series is based on the original concept of Judy Mazzeo Zocchi.

ART DIRECTION
Barbie Lambert & Rizco Design
DESIGN
Rizco Design
EDITED BY
Andrea Curley
PROJECT MANAGER
Lisa Aldorasi
EDUCATIONAL CONSULTANT
Maura Ruane McKenna
PRE-PRESS BY
Pixel Graphics

EXPLORE THE LETTERS OF THE ALPHABET WITH MY LETTER LIBRARY*

Aimee's **A** Book
Bebe's **B** Book
Cassie's **C** Book
Delia's **D** Book
Emma's **E** Book
Faye's **F** Book
George's **G** Book
Henry's **H** Book
Izzy's **I** Book
Jade's **J** Book
Kelsey's **K** Book
Logan's **L** Book
Mia's **M** Book
Nate's **N** Book
Owen's **O** Book
Peter's **P** Book
Quinn's **Q** Book
Rosie's **R** Book
Sofie's **S** Book
Tad's **T** Book
Uri's **U** Book
Vera's **V** Book
Will's **W** Book
Xavia's **X** Book
Yola's **Y** Book
Zach's **Z** Book

* All titles also available in bilingual English/Spanish versions.

WEBSITE
www.dingles.com
E-MAIL
info@dingles.com

Dd

My Letter Library leads young children through the alphabet one letter at a time. By focusing on an individual letter in each book, the series allows youngsters to identify and absorb the concept of each letter thoroughly before being introduced to the next. In addition, it invites them to look around and discover where objects beginning with the specific letter appear in their own world.

A a B b C c **D d** E e F f G g

H h I i J j K k L l M m N n

O o P p Q q R r S s T t U u

V v W w X x Y y Z z

D is for Delia.

Delia is a dainty donkey.

At Delia's backyard picnic
you will find **d**aisies,

Dd

some **d**affodils
standing tall,

Dd

and three fluffy **d**andelions.

Dd

While picnicking with Delia
you can eat a **d**oughnut,

Dd

share a delicious plate

of **d**esserts,

Dd

or nibble a **d**rumstick
that her mother prepared.

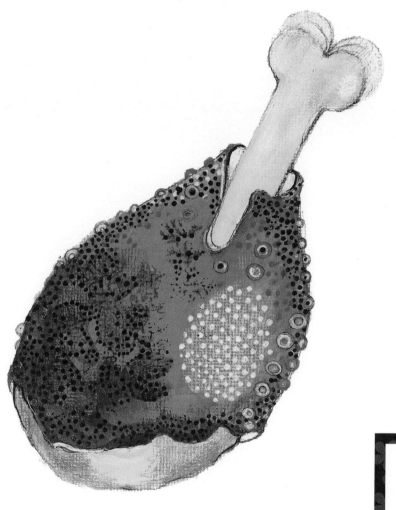

Dd

During Delia's picnic
you can play with **d**ominoes,

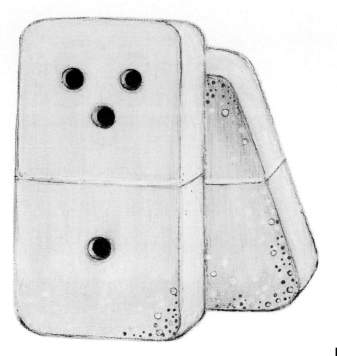

Dd

dance with a **d**oll,

Dd

or make music

with a **d**rum.

Dd

Things that begin with
the letter **D** are all around.

DAISIES

DAFFODILS

DANDELIONS

DOUGHNUT

DESSERTS

DRUMSTICK

DOMINOES

DOLL

DRUM

Where at Delia's picnic
can they be found?

Have a **"D"** Day!

Read "D" stories all day long.
Read books about donkeys, flowers such as daisies or daffodils, dolls, and other **D** words. Then have the child pick out all of the words and pictures starting with the letter **D**.

Make a "D" Craft: A Dinosaur
Staple two pieces of 12-x-18-inch construction paper together.

Trace a dinosaur shape on one of the pieces. Draw eyes and a mouth, and write the letter **D** on its chest.

Have the child cut out the dinosaur shape and the other paper together.

Staple the two shapes together along the edge, but leave an opening.

Stuff the dinosaur with cotton balls. Then staple the opening closed and enjoy the **"D"** dinosaur!

Make a "D" Snack: Dirt Cups
- Fill two-thirds of a cup with chocolate pudding and place a layer of crushed chocolate cookies on top.
- Place gummy worms on top of the cookies and cover them with more cookies.
- Chill and enjoy!

For additional **"D"** Day ideas and a reading list, go to www.dingles.com.

About **Letters**

Use the My Letter Library series to teach a child to identify letters and recognize the sounds they make by hearing them used and repeated in each story.

Ask:

- What letter is this book about?
- Can you name all of the **D** pictures on each page?
- Which **D** picture is your favorite? Why?
- Can you find all of the words in this book that begin with the letter **D**?

ENVIRONMENT

Discuss objects that begin with the letter **D** in the child's immediate surroundings and environment.

Use these questions to further the conversation:

- Have you ever been on a picnic? If so, did you have fun?
- If you go on another picnic, what food beginning with the letter **D** would you bring along?
- Would you bring some toys like Delia did?
- What **D** toys would you bring?
- What is your favorite dessert?

OBSERVATIONS

The My Letter Library series can be used to enhance the child's imagination. Encourage the child to look around and tell you what he or she sees.

Ask:

- Have you ever had a pretend picnic in your room?
- If so, who were your guests?
- What is your favorite **D** object at home? Why?
- Where do donkeys live?

TRY SOMETHING NEW...

Help your parent pack a picnic lunch. Find someplace fun to have your picnic (for example, at the beach, a park, or a playground).

J. L. MAZZEO grew up in Middletown, New Jersey, as part of a close-knit Italian American family. She currently resides in Monmouth County, New Jersey, and still remains close to family members in heart and home.

HELEN ROSS REVUTSKY was born in St. Petersburg, Russia, where she received a degree in stage artistry/ design. She worked as the directing artist in Kiev's famous Governmental Puppet Theatre. Her first book, *I Can Read the Alphabet,* was published in Moscow in 1998. Helen now lives in London, where she has illustrated several children's books.